FAMILIAR

JEREMY C. SHIPP

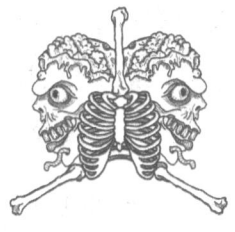

Ghoulish Books
San Antonio, Texas

Familiar

ISBN: 978-1-963801-02-6

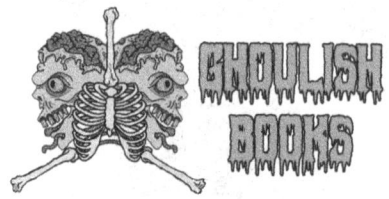

www.Ghoulish.rip

Cover Art by Betty Rocksteady

Also by Jeremy C. Shipp:

To all the weird sisters out there
brewing trouble

THE **HOSTESS** with the wide-set eyes doesn't ask me where I'd like to be seated. She knows me enough to instantly head out of the bustling restaurant to the edge of the floating patio, next to the water.

"Your waiter will be right with you," she says, an undercurrent of gloom in her voice. I feel a sudden urge to ask her what's wrong, but I don't know how she would react to that. We're strangers, after all.

"Thank you," I say.

While I'm waiting for Eva, I order drinks for the two of us. I sip at a mimosa and try to clear my mind of everything I should be thinking about.

Near me, a girl and her little brother lean far over the railing and drop Tylenol-sized pellets into the lake. Hundreds of catfish swarm beside the children, poking their heads into the air, opening and closing their mouths.

"That pellet wasn't for you," the girl says to one of the fish. "Don't be so greedy."

I look out across the lake. Canoes and kayaks slide across the scintillating waters. In the distance, I spot some dark mass breaking the surface and then disappearing just as quickly. I know that's only driftwood or some other bit of debris out there, but the dark mass still makes me think of the monster of the lake and all its many forms. According to my dad, the monster was a sea serpent back when he was a kid. When I was young, we talked about a giant salamander in the lake. Nowadays, kids say the monster is a large frog with a human face.

A high-pitched scream causes me to jump a little. For a second I'm afraid that one of the kids fell into the water with all those squirming catfish. But I look over, and I find the kids throwing gummy worms at each other's open mouths. The boy throws a worm over his sister's head into the water and he screams again. "Stop wasting them," the sister says.

FAMILIAR

I take a deep breath, trying to calm myself down. I'm definitely on edge today.

I decide that as soon as Eva shows up, I'll tell her that I don't want to discuss Gordon this morning. I want this to be like one of our bygone brunches, where we laughed and talked about novels and irritating co-workers and whatever the hell else we used to think about.

"I'm starved," Eva says, from somewhere behind me. "I could eat a hippo."

"You're twenty minutes late," I say.

"Sorry." My sister takes a seat at the table and grabs for her drink with both hands. "I saw that our favorite hostess is working today."

"Yeah," I say. "Did she seem sad to you?"

"I didn't notice," Eva says, while holding her glass to her mouth, like some ventriloquist performer. Then she carefully sets her drink on the table. "But I'm sure you're right. Maybe we should invite her somewhere to cheer her up. And by we, I mean you."

"Nope," I say. "I've been asked out when I'm working, and it's shitty. I'm not doing that to her."

"I'd agree with you, except she obviously likes you. This isn't some I'm-being-paid-to-be-nice-to-you situation. This is a love story waiting to happen. Just leave your number on a napkin and write 'for the hostess with beautiful eyes' and see what happens."

"You're delusional."

The waiter soon materializes and asks if we both want our usual. We do.

As soon as our plates arrive, Eva says, "Fuck ambrosia. Pancakes are the food of the gods." She lifts a large hunk of syrup-soaked pancake to her mouth, but her fork slips from her fingers before she can take a bite. The fork hits the edge of the table and clatters on the ground.

I sigh. "You drank the liquid again last night. You promised me you wouldn't drink it so often."

"I promised that I'd consider not drinking it so often." She picks up her spoon. "But I'm fine. Just a little groggy."

"You can barely keep your eyes open. How many drops did you take?"

"Twelve, I think."

"Jesus, Eva."

She shrugs almost imperceptibly. "The effects will wear off. What's important is that I had a dream last night that I need to tell you about." She lifts a large chunk of pancake balanced precariously on her spoon, and this time she manages not to drop anything. "It was about you and me and Gordon," she says, with her mouth full. After she swallows, she says, "You were almost yourself, except you had this vibrant red hair. It was almost too vibrant, really, like you were in a Technicolor film." She stares at my hair in silence for a few seconds and then meets my eyes. "Gordon was a smooth river stone with googly eyes and a mouth and little chicken legs." She slowly lifts her arm again, and the scrambled eggs jiggle a little at the end of the spoon. "So I was sitting on the couch with Gordon curled up on my lap when you got a phone call. You learned that we were being kicked out of our apartment immediately. We only had time to grab a few things before we had to leave. You took your laptop, and I took this weird painting of a crab, and Gordon carried a squeak toy in his mouth. I think the toy was shaped like a bone."

Eva takes a large gulp of her second mimosa.

She continues, "The three of us got into a van with black windows and we were taken to this high-rise apartment tower with crumbling concrete walls and boarded-up windows. I felt sick to my stomach the moment I saw the place." She sighs, and she stares out at the lake. "Things only got worse when we checked out our new apartment. There was trash all over the floor. Moldy banana peels and grimy socks and wet magazines. The place smelled like the worst BO you can imagine. As soon as we walked in, you started sobbing. Gordon chewed on his bone nervously, making it squeak over and over. It was irritating as hell, and I asked him to stop, but he wouldn't. I walked over to the window, hoping we at least had a nice view of the city. All I could see outside though were greenish-yellow flies the size of tennis balls. They kept slamming against the window, trying to get in. The glass was cracked all over. It was only a matter of time before they broke through."

I set my fork on my napkin. "What a perfect story to tell over brunch."

Eva ignores me. She continues to stare at the lake. "I didn't think things could get any worse, but then a blast of wind rattled the windows. The wind sort of growled, louder and louder, and we could feel the apartment moving. I realized that the whole high-rise was swaying in the wind. You kept saying we were going to die, and Gordon ran around in circles, squeaking and slipping on banana peels. It wasn't funny at the time. I wanted to comfort both of you and tell you that everything was going to turn out fine, but I was pretty sure you were right. I thought we were going to die." She returns her attention to her

Brunchstravaganza Platter. "Eventually, though, the wind died down, and Gordon scratched at the front door with his little chicken foot, like he wanted to go out. So I opened the door for him. He stepped out and looked back, like he wanted us to follow him. So we did. He led us down the hall to an old-fashioned elevator with a rusty, wrought iron door. We stepped inside and I pulled a lever and we ascended, slowly. The elevator squeaked and groaned." While she speaks, she uses her spoon to show the progression of the elevator. "Every so often, we dropped for a few seconds, and you screamed, and I was half-positive we would fall to our deaths. But we never did. We kept rising, and I was a little afraid of what we might find at the top. I thought the wind might cause the tower to lean so far over that we'd fall off. I thought we might get attacked by those flies. But when we reached the top, we stepped out of the elevator, and there wasn't any wind, and there weren't any flies. It was dark out, and the sky was filled with light. There were stars, and meteors, and comets, and enormous planets with sparkling rings and swirling atmospheres. I'm getting goosebumps just thinking about it. See?" She holds out her arm and then gently rubs the goosebumps with her hand. "I'm sure you understand what I'm saying here."

"No, I don't," I say, although that's not exactly true. I can tell where she's going with this, more or less.

"We're in the tower," Eva says. "You're afraid of taking that next step with Gordon. And I guess I am too. But we don't need to be. We're heading toward something amazing."

"You don't know that."

"I wish I could show you what it was like up there." She points her spoon at me. "You should take some of the liquid tonight. Maybe you'll see it."

"That's not the kind of thing that I see. You know that."

"Yeah." She studies me carefully and I suddenly feel self-conscious. "Anyway, I think we're ready to move forward. I'm ready, at least. What do you think?"

"I don't know," I say. "I'll think about it."

Eva smiles at me a little, and for a while, we eat in silence. I look out at the lake. In my mind, the twinkling specks of sunlight on the water become stars. I'm on the tower now, looking up, as the universe swirls around me in streaks of blazing reds and blues and yellows. For a moment, I connect with whatever Eva connected with last night, and I get goosebumps. After that moment, the daydream dissipates. But the meaning of Eva's vision remains inside me, humming like a power line.

THREE DAYS LATER, and I make my decision. And we go out. Eva wanders the streets of downtown for two hours and thirty-eight minutes before the man in the leather cowboy hat starts following her. I trail the two of them from afar. By now, tailing people without being noticed comes as second nature to me. In my dreams, the man was nothing but a smear of colors. In real life, he's a man in his forties or fifties in a well-tailored suit and a white dress shirt with an unbuttoned collar.

I call Eva and as soon she picks up, I say, "He's here. He's following you."

"Okay," Eva says, quietly. I detect a hint of fear in her voice. That's not something that happens very often.

"Everything's going to be fine," I say. "Do you know how to get to the alley from here?"

"No. I don't know how to get anywhere from anywhere."

That's only a slight exaggeration,

really. She might have the worst sense of direction in the world.

"Turn right on Green Street," I say. "That's coming up in two blocks."

"Can you still see me?"

"Yeah. I won't lose you. I'll call you back if anything changes. Remember to turn right on Green Street."

"Okay."

I hang up. On the opposite side of the street, Eva hangs up as well. Cowboy Hat continues to follow her, only a few yards behind her. He moves with the same confident gait as the blurred man from my dreams. While he watches her, he rubs at his earhole with his thumb.

Eva turns right on Green Street, then walks into the alley we chose three days ago. Cowboy Hat pauses for only a moment before following her into the narrow passageway. My heart slams against my chest.

I want to run after them, but I might scare Cowboy Hat away.

I cross the street, slowly, gripping my

phone in my hand. Something's wrong. Eva should have called me by now. I walk faster. My face burns with dread.

Before I reach the alley, my phone buzzes silently in my hand.

"Eva?" I say.

"Everything's fine," she says. "Come on over."

She hangs up, and I enter the alley, passing stacks of water-damaged newspapers and magazines. Cowboy Hat's standing in the middle of the passageway, with his hands at his sides, staring directly at the withered eyeball in Eva's hand.

Eva smiles at me. "It works," she says.

She lifts the eyeball over her head, and Cowboy Hat tilts his head upward slightly. When Eva lowers her arm again, Cowboy Hat lowers his head.

"So I walked in here and I turned around and he smiled at me, sort of nervously, like he was embarrassed. He tugged at his right ear, the way you said he would. He's definitely the man from your dream. Don't you think?"

"I think so."

"Anyway, he said something about how I shouldn't walk through the city without a protector. With every word, he kept stepping closer. As soon as he got close enough, I took out the eye and I told him to look at it. He did." She relates this to me, quietly. I don't need these details, but that never stops her from talking.

"Good job," I say. "Should we head home, or do you need a minute?"

"I'm ready. I'm fine."

We head towards our apartment complex, with Eva in the lead. She keeps the eyeball in her hand, with the golden iris pointed behind her. Cowboy Hat ambles after her with an awkward, toddler-like gait. We've found that once you're in the thrall of the eye, you feel extremely uncomfortable if you're farther than four feet away from it. So Cowboy Hat stays close.

I take up the rear, with my hand in my jacket pocket, gripping my pepper spray.

After a couple blocks, Eva stops and turns around. "I really need to pee."

"We're almost home," I say. "We're literally ten minutes away."

"I can't wait ten minutes, Char. I'm going to explode. I'm not kidding." She holds out the eyeball. "Here. I'll be right back."

I take the eyeball, carefully. I make sure that Cowboy Hat can see the iris at all times during the handover.

After Eva rushes off into an indie bookstore, I lead Cowboy Hat toward a brick wall, away from all this foot traffic. On my way to the wall, someone steps right in front of me and yells, "Char!"

I almost drop the eyeball. "Titus," I say, and I can feel a frosty bead of sweat running down my back.

Titus grins and gives me a thumbs up. The banana on his t-shirt is also grinning and giving me a thumbs up. The text bubble above the banana reads "Tell me I'm a peeling."

"Did you see my shirt?" Titus says.

"Yeah. That's funny."

At this point, Titus looks down at the eyeball in my hand. Then Titus looks at

Cowboy Hat while Cowboy Hat stares expressionlessly at the eye. The entranced man sways from side to side, his legs buckling a little every few seconds.

I say, "We're um . . . we're doing this weird scavenger hunt. We have to find bizarre items and then accomplish certain tasks with them. Right now, Carl has to stare at this eyeball for fifteen minutes without saying a word."

"Wow," Titus says, smiling again. "That sounds like a hoot. Can anyone join this thing?"

"Actually, the . . . the enrollment period is over for this year."

"But I could join next year, yeah?"

"No, I'm afraid this is the last year."

"Damn. That's a shame. Well, have fun." He pats Cowboy Hat hard on the shoulder, causing him to stumble forward. Cowboy Hat makes a sound somewhere between a gurgle and a scream.

I squat down and reposition the eye quickly. Cowboy Hat breathes fast, his nostrils flaring.

"Oops, sorry," Titus says. "I guess I don't know my own strength. You alright, Carl?"

"He's fine," I say. "He can't talk, remember?"

"Oh right. Well, good luck."

Once Titus walks away, I take a deep breath.

In another minute, Eva returns. "I feel reborn."

I spend the walk home worrying Cowboy Hat is on the verge of breaking free of the thrall. I'm afraid that his flaring nostrils and his twitching fingers mean that the eye is losing its grip on him. I almost bring all this up with Eva, but in the end, I keep my worries to myself. If he does break free, we'll handle it.

Thankfully, we reach our apartment without any further hiccups.

Eva tosses her jacket onto the dining table and says, "I'm ravenous. Can we order pizza when we're finished? Are you in a pizza mood?"

"Sure," I say, but honestly, nothing sounds appetizing.

I'm still worried about Cowboy Hat breaking free, and so I want to get this done and over with right now. I lead him into the living room, over to the far wall.

"Gordon, we did it," Eva says.

Gordon clicks his teeth together a few times in excitement.

Then the four of us stand together in silence for a while.

"So," Eva says. "How exactly do we do this? Do we just . . . put him in?"

"I think so. In my dreams, we always put in his right hand, but I'm not sure if that's important."

"Do you want me to do it?"

"Yeah."

I use the eyeball to position Cowboy Hat as close to the wall as possible. Eva then grabs Cowboy Hat's wrist and slowly pushes his right hand into Gordon's open mouth.

"Is this okay, Gordon?" Eva says.

The corners of Gordon's mouth turn up in a small smile.

"Can I let him go now?" Eva says.

"Yeah," I say.

Eva lets go of Cowboy Hat's wrist and then backs away a few steps.

After a few seconds, Cowboy Hat collapses to his knees, his hand still held inside Gordon's mouth. Cowboy Hat's head tilts to the side, resting against his shoulder.

I move the eyeball out of Cowboy Hat's line of sight, and he remains in the exact same position. So I put the eyeball away in my jacket pocket. I take a deep breath.

"What now?" Eva says.

"I could use a break," I say. "Cowboy Hat should be secure for now. Do you want to order those pizzas?"

Eva immediately dashes away, saying, "I could eat an elephant made of pepperoni."

Before letting myself turn away, I scrutinize the scene in front of me one last time. Cowboy Hat's nostrils aren't flaring anymore. His fingers aren't twitching. Gordon's making a soft slurping sound as he gradually sucks Cowboy Hat's arm deeper inside him.

"Are you alright, Gordon?" I say.

But Gordon doesn't smile or frown or respond in any way. He seems too absorbed in what he's doing to hear me.

I walk away.

As soon as I sit on the couch, a wave of exhaustion rushes through me. I'd like to play some old movie on the TV and fall asleep right here and now, but I can't. We're not done yet.

I mess around on my phone for a bit, then Eva comes over from the kitchen and hands me a mug of coffee that says "#2 sister" in gold glitter. She grins.

"Thanks," I say.

Eva sinks into her velvety, purple recliner. She stirs her coffee with a spoon, clinking the inside of the mug over and over. "You know, I can't believe we're actually doing this. I know I gave you all those little speeches about how this is our destiny and shit, but I thought you would chicken out. And I thought I would chicken out if you chickened out. But we're actually doing this."

"Could you stop clinking your spoon? I have a headache."

"Sorry."

For a while, I sip my perfect cup of coffee in silence. I'm not looking at Eva, but I can feel her eyes searching the side of my face. I can also feel the air thickening around us with a dense, staticky energy, emanating from the far wall.

The pizza arrives quickly, and we half-watch a TV show about a British puppeteer who solves crimes. In this episode, the puppeteer uses his powers of ventriloquism to convince a bank heist team that they're being haunted by the ghost of a dead pirate captain. Sometimes, during the quieter moments of the show, I can hear Cowboy Hat murmuring.

After the show finishes, I carry our dishes to the sink, and I feel almost as if I'm moving through water.

"So," Eva says, standing. "Should we finish this?"

"Yeah."

We return to the far wall of the living

room and we stare silently at the scene. Cowboy Hat dangles limply from Gordon's mouth, his right arm almost completely lost inside Gordon's throat, or whatever exists beyond Gordon's mouth.

I kneel down next to Cowboy Hat and say, "You don't want to harm anyone else."

"I woh," Cowboy Hat says. "I won't hah."

"You don't want to harm anyone else," Eva says.

"I won't harm anyone again," he says.

"You won't remember us," I say. "But our words will live in your soul until the day you die."

"Until the day I die," he says.

Suddenly, Gordon spits out Cowboy Hat. The man collapses to the carpet and releases a long, muted moan. He's now missing the majority of his right arm. Somehow, he's not bleeding. Gordon must have sealed up the wound.

Eva says, "I thought Gordon was only going to take his hand."

"That's how it was when I saw it," I say. "Gordon must have needed more."

FAMILIAR

I take the eyeball out of my jacket pocket, and as soon as Cowboy Hat focuses on the object, we lead him back to the alley.

When I release him from our thrall, he looks around nervously. He glances in our direction and doesn't seem to register us at all.

Once the alley is long behind us, Eva says, "Fuck. We did it."

We did.

I follow Eva up the stairs to our apartment, so that I can cry silently behind her. I'm relieved that we survived all this. I'm happy that I'll never dream of this particular blurred man ever again. But for the most part, these are not tears of joy. We're still in the tower, far from the stars and meteors and comets and planets. I don't know what's to come. But according to that scrawny, quivery part of my soul that's never wrong, the next hunt will be much worse.

WHILE PRETENDING TO be asleep in my bed, I watch my sister and her boyfriend as they stand in silence, side-by-side, staring at the living room wall. Marcus hunches up his shoulders and squeezes his hands into fists. Eva doesn't so much turn as spin to look at him. She's smiling. Somehow, she thinks this will turn out well.

Marcus says something, then walks away from the wall, now facing my bedroom. I close my eyes.

After a few seconds, I can hear them. They must be standing in the kitchen.

"He's a good person," Eva says.

"Person?" Marcus says, quietly. He only speaks this softly when he's angry.

"Or whatever he is," Eva says. "He's good."

"And how do you know that exactly? You said he doesn't talk."

I open my eyes again. I can see Gordon

frowning from here. His teeth shimmer in the lamplight.

"He communicates in different ways," Eva says. "You can stand by the wall and you can feel his, you know, beneficence. I'll show you." She pulls Marcus by the hand, into my view, but he yanks away and returns to the kitchen.

"Oh, fuck no," he says. "I'm not getting anywhere near that thing."

"He's not a thing."

"He's a fucking mouth in the wall."

Eva stares at him, her hands slowly opening and closing. "I shared this with you because I thought you were open-minded. I *know* you're open-minded. You always talk about how much you want to see an alien, or a ghost, or bigfoot. I thought you would be excited to meet him."

Marcus steps into my view, closer to Eva. I can see sweat glistening on his forehead. Beyond him, Gordon's mouth opens wide.

"This thing is different," Marcus says.

"It's fucking bizarre. Even you can see that, can't you?"

"You don't know him," Eva says. "You haven't even given him a chance."

Marcus presses his hand against the side of his face. "The worst part about all this is that you're so confident you're right. That's what scares me. That's what tells me you're not being cautious enough. You're jumping into something you don't understand, because that's what you always do. You do realize that, don't you?"

"That's enough," Eva says. "Go home and cool down. I'll explain more about all this when you're ready to listen to me."

"I'm not leaving you alone with it," Marcus says.

"I'm not alone, and you know that. If you leave now, we'll have a nice, long conversation in a few hours, and we'll work this all out peacefully. If you refuse to leave, I'll break up with you and I'll kick you out anyway. Either way, you're going home."

"Damn it, Eva. I'm not trying to piss

you off. I'm scared for you. You understand that, don't you?"

"*You understand that, don't you?*" she mimics. "That's so fucking patronizing. I hate when you say that."

"Okay. Okay, I'm going." Marcus sighs loud enough for even me to hear. "If anything happens, call me. I'll come right back."

Once Marcus leaves, Eva stands there for a while, staring at the door. A few yards behind her, Gordon opens his mouth wider than ever before, like a serpent with an unhinged jaw. He's almost ready.

Eva drifts into my room. "Did you hear any of that?"

"Yeah."

She sits on the edge of my bed, on a square of my quilt with appliqué moonflowers and kangaroo rats. For a second, I see my grandma's face materialize vaguely in a dark corner of the room.

"I didn't think he'd react this way," Eva says. She falls onto her back into a position that looks uncomfortable, with her legs still dangling to the floor. She gazes at the ceiling, barely blinking.

"He's freaking out," I say. "We freaked out a little the first time we saw Gordon."

"Yeah."

"Maybe he'll come around."

"Yeah." She sits up again. "I'll text him and explain everything. I'll tell him about my dream with the tower. I'll tell him about Cowboy Hat. Do you really think he'll come around?"

"Maybe," I say, and I want to believe that. I hope Marcus surprises me.

I open my mouth to reassure her more emphatically, but a booming thud resonates from the other room. The sound smashes against me hard and swirls around inside my chest.

"It's Gordon," I say. "I think he finished disgorging."

Eva dashes away, and after a few moments, she returns holding a shriveled, severed hand with golden veins visible through the almost-transparent skin.

"Don't let it drip on the quilt," I say.

"I wasn't going to," Eva says. She sits on the edge of the bed, holding the hand over the fake hardwood floor.

"What do you think it does?" Eva says.

"I don't know," I say. "I'm sure he'll tell us eventually."

With a paper towel, Eva carefully wipes off the hand. "Maybe it'll grant us wishes, like in that monkey paw story. Maybe we'll be able to stop the blurred ones all at once."

"Do you remember how the wishes turned out in that story?"

"Sort of. But maybe this is a nice magical hand, without a duplicitous bone in her body."

"Right."

Eva tosses the crumpled-up paper towel at the small trash can by my desk and misses.

"Eva," I say.

"Sorry," she says, heading over to the towel. "I'm going to text Marcus. Do you want me to leave the hand?"

"No."

I close my eyes and listen to Eva's soft footsteps as she darts away. The darkness behind my eyelids becomes more pronounced when Eva turns off the ceiling light in the living room. The darkness streams inside me from all sides.

Soon, I'm looking for someone, pointing my flashlight out at the lake, illuminating empty canoes and kayaks and rowboats. Starlight glimmers on the water. If I look carefully, I can see a chubby moon reflected there. I can see planets, green and yellow and reddish-orange. They remind me of spring. In the distance, a dark mass emerges from the lake, and as soon as I shine my flashlight on his face, he swiftly submerges himself again. Am I here looking for the monster? No, I'm here for the hostess with the elfish face. I wrote a letter to her, didn't I, and she wrote back to me, asking to meet me here tonight. What if she hasn't shown herself because she's in trouble?

Feeling slightly frantic, I point my

flashlight randomly in various directions. The blazing blue beam of my flashlight wakes up an enormous owl, who bares his fangs at me and hisses. Near me, thousands of catfish thrust their heads out of the water, opening and closing their humanlike lips, murmuring, begging for worms.

"I don't have any," I say.

Suddenly, one of the catfish explodes, and I wake up.

I can't see much, but I can make out someone standing in the living room, facing the far wall. The silhouette doesn't look at all like Eva. The shadow-figure lifts an object over his shoulder and smashes the wall with a sound like shattering glass.

"Stop," I say. "Stop!"

I grab the withered eye from the wooden box in my sock drawer, and I rush into the living room.

"Stop," I say.

Marcus ignores me and raises the mallet again.

After sprinting up beside him, I hold the eye in front of his face.

He freezes.

"Eva!" I say, and then I turn my attention back to Marcus. I don't know what I'm doing. I don't have anything close to a plan. "I'll release you, but you need to promise me you'll put down the mallet."

His nostrils flare, the corners of his mouth twitching upward in an angry grin.

"Promise me," I say.

A few seconds later, he manages a small spasm of a nod.

I lower the eyeball, and Marcus lowers the mallet.

"It doesn't matter what you do," he says. "I'm already done."

"Give me your key," I say, and he obeys.

Once he's gone, I turn to the wound in the wall where Gordon used to be. Gordon must have changed the molecular structure of the wall, because the fragments on the floor don't look like drywall at all. The fragments are small and thin, like pieces of broken slate. I pick through the wreckage, cutting up my fingers, searching for any sign of Gordon. I can't find his lips or his tongue or his large, light-blue teeth. He's gone.

I wander into Eva's room and yell her name.

She remains motionless as a corpse, which means that she took at least ten drops of the liquid before bed. Now I won't be able to wake her until morning.

In bed again, I stare into the darkest corner of the room where my grandma showed herself, but the shadows don't coalesce again. I peer into the living room at the spot where Gordon used to reside.

After I close my eyes, the hole in the wall follows me into my dreams. There's a hole in a skyscraper. Men and women in black suits sit at the edges of their offices, dangling their legs a thousand feet in the air. One man loses a shoe, and a woman next to him laughs and waves down at the leather oxford as it falls.

There's a hole in my grandma's house. I'm in the living room, sitting on my flattened bean bag chair with a book on my lap. Through a gaping, ragged opening in the wall, I see yuccas and apricot mallows and a prickly pear cactus with magenta flowers.

"What if the animals come in?" I say, but there's no one else around to answer me.

There's a hole in the lake. There's a hole in the water, and when I peek inside, I expect to see a sea serpent or a giant salamander or a frog with a human face. But he's only a man with a goatee, his fingers squeezing the neck of the hostess. She looks up at me, begging for help without speaking a word.

"Hold on," I say.

But I'm already somewhere new. I'm floating among the stars and meteors and comets, reaching a withered hand out towards Earth, and there's a hole in the world.

EVA TOUCHES THE jagged edge of the opening Marcus created before I can stop her. Blood blooms on her fingertip.

"Be careful," I say, too late. I'm always too late. Even as kids, I said "be careful" after she leapt off a swing or broke a window or defied our father.

Eva disturbs the pile of bizarre drywall shards on the floor with her puffy penguin slipper and then faces me, sucking on her bloody finger.

"Huh," she says.

"Wow," I say. "You seem truly devastated."

Eva sits on her recliner and puts her feet up on the coffee table. I sigh. That was Grandma's coffee table. I wish Eva would treat Grandma's possessions, or ex-possessions I should say, with more respect.

"Don't get me wrong," Eva says. "I'm

pissed off at Marcus, but I don't think this changes anything."

"How does it not?" I say. "Marcus destroyed Gordon, or he destroyed the spot in our reality where Gordon can show himself. Either way, we're alone in this now, and we're going to run out of the liquid. We can't progress without the liquid."

Eva wraps her finger with an old napkin from the coffee table. "I know I don't have your skills when it comes to foresight, but I can feel where we are right now, and we're still in that high-rise apartment tower. When I close my eyes, your hair is still that vibrant red. I didn't remember this until a few days ago, but one summer when we stayed at Grandma's house, we wandered around every day, and we collected things. One day, we were sitting on our bean bag chairs, half-watching some cartoon, half-looking through our cardboard box of treasures from the desert. And you told me that you wanted hair like the red flowers we found.

FAMILIAR

You wanted eyes hard and blue like our chrysocolla stone. You wanted skin like our dead painted lady butterfly. It was all nonsense, sort of, but it also wasn't. We were happy those summers, and it was more than happiness. We were strong. We could feel things. Grandma started us on the path that we're on now, and even when we were kids, you knew where we were headed." Eva unwraps her finger and tosses the bloodied napkin into a dirty cereal bowl. "When I close my eyes, you're made of flowers and stones and butterflies, and we're still in the apartment from my dream. The wind's growling, and the high-rise is swaying in the wind, and Gordon's running and slipping on banana peels. We're afraid this is the end, but it's not. We'll get through this."

I sigh and pick up the dirty cereal bowl. "I told you I wanted flower hair, and stone eyes, and butterfly skin because I was trying to make you laugh. I also told you I wanted to replace my brain with old bottle caps. It didn't mean anything."

Eva looks up at me and frowns slightly. For a moment, she looks like she might cry, but she doesn't. She grabs the remote.

I head into the kitchen and start washing dishes and tincture bottles. What feels like a cold stone wall presses against my chest. I wish I could do more for Eva. I wish I could convince her to grieve now for Gordon and for the end of our silly aspirations. But I don't have that kind of power. Every day, she'll wait for Gordon to come back, and every day she'll lose a little bit of hope. She'll let herself suffer.

Sometimes I wish Eva would stop seeing hope in every loss and every broken thing, but then again, if she didn't, she wouldn't be Eva.

LIKE EVERY MORNING these days, I step out of my bedroom and immediately glance at the still unpainted patch of drywall in the living room. My heart still aches a little at the sight. I miss Gordon. I didn't know him the way a human being knows another person. He wouldn't, or couldn't explain what he was or where he came from. The concept of self seemed to baffle him somewhat. He didn't even have a name when we first met him. Sometimes, in an attempt to help me understand him better, he let me dream his dreams. He showed me visions of shifting flesh and phantasmagorical colors. These images, of course, didn't mean much of anything to me. But despite our missteps and mistranslations, I did come to understand pieces of his heart. His energy was, as Eva likes to say, beneficent.

These are the thoughts I like to think to myself so that I can pretend that my grief is some pure, selfless thing. But as I'm sitting on the couch, sipping my coffee, I can feel shame heating up my face. The truth is that part of me is glad that Gordon's dead, or gone. I can't help it. I'm happy. Part of me wanted off of the high-rise apartment tower from the beginning. I don't want to face greenish-yellow flies the size of tennis balls or lake monsters with magicians' goatees. I don't want to stand at the top of the tower with a body made of desert, blessed by a swirling, blazing universe. I don't need that kind of responsibility in my life.

Eva yawns behind me, and I quickly turn away from the drywall, trying and probably failing not to look guilty. Luckily, Eva's still half-asleep. She heads into the kitchen, stumbling for a moment on nothing at all.

"You're up early," I say.

Eva jumps at the sound of my voice. "Yeah," she says, and swigs directly from the bottle of cold brew concentrate. "Work needs me early."

"You know you can't lie," I say. "I don't know why you're even trying."

"Fine," she says, tossing the bottle back in the fridge. "I'm going to meet Marcus. I didn't want to tell you because I didn't want to see that apocalyptic look on your face. It's too early in the morning to deal with faces like that."

I try to morph my face into something less stern. "I'm worried about you. That's all. You didn't see Marcus with the mallet."

"He explained things to me last night." Eva pulls a pair of neon socks out of her jacket pocket and begins the awkward process of putting them on without sitting. "When Marcus was five or six, he was playing by himself in the front yard, and a dog approached him and bit his face. He remembers the dog as being the size of a bus. He remembers the teeth like they were kitchen knives. He still has the scars under his beard. And he still has a thing about teeth. He says that after he saw Gordon, he panicked. He made a mistake."

"Gordon might be dead," I say. "That's more than a mistake."

"Gordon's a mystical being," Eva says, almost falling over. "I don't think a tiny mallet is enough to kill him."

"And what if you're wrong? What if Marcus killed him?"

Eva rushes past me and slips her shoes on by the front door. "Marcus thought he was saving us," she says. "He's a better person than you think."

"Right."

Eva faces me and says, "A few weeks ago, we watched this commercial where a little girl left her stuffed elephant out in the rain, and Marcus cried. Sometimes he makes me these little penguins out of clay, with sun hats and bow ties and canes. With each penguin, he gives me a laminated notecard that shows their name and blood type and likes and dislikes."

"You don't have to tell me all this," I say.

"Yes, I do. You think you have him all figured out. You think you figured him out after the first five minutes you met him. You could at least give him a chance."

"Sorry if I seem a little irritated. I guess that's what happens when someone kills one of my friends."

"Gordon isn't dead," Eva yells. She grabs her purse and storms out of the apartment.

The moment she's gone, I already regret the entire conversation. Why do I attack her when she's at her weakest? Why am I like this?

I sit on the velvety recliner, sipping at my imperfect cup of coffee. Eva's coffee always tastes so much better. I should tell her how much I love her coffee.

Sighing, I look over at the patch of unpainted drywall. "Can you hear me?" I say, to the empty room.

Of course, no one replies.

With a trembling hand, I drip the last eighteen drops of the liquid into my mouth, coating my tongue with the taste of roses and ozone. If Eva could see me now, a mischievous grin would spread across her face, as if to say, "Who's the wild one now?"

I have never taken anything close to eighteen drops before, and for good reason. My visions are not like Eva's. But I feel, instinctively, that if I'm ever going to speak to Gordon again, I need to act rashly. Stupidly.

The truth is that, more than anything, I need to reach the top of the high-rise apartment tower to see the stars and meteors and planets. As a girl, when I told Eva that I wanted butterfly skin and chrysocolla stone eyes, I was only partially joking. All these dreams and visions and metaphors represent something that I don't understand, but their truth crackles inside my chest like a bonfire.

Through my closed eyelids, I see my grandma's sturdy legs, bestrewn with blue veins like streaks of lightning. Towering over me, she places a paper plate on the carpet. I'm sitting on my bean bag chair, leaning my head to the side so that I can continue to watch the TV. Flesh contorts on the screen. Colors swirl and undulate. My grandma walks away, and I look down at the paper plate. There's a slice of hot rye bread with a swirly symbol in the middle, drawn in thick, violet icing.

I take a bite of the bread, and the icing tastes strangely like roses. I look over to ask Eva if her bread tastes right, but her bean bag chair is empty.

Grandma's no longer in the kitchen.

I'm a little girl, but I still remember the eighteen drops that I took before bed at some point in the distant future. I'm frightened that the blurred men will arrive at any moment. I'm frightened that there will be too many of them.

On the TV screen, brutish-looking faces stretch and gnarl.

I eat the rest of my bread, because Grandma always says that the symbol will protect us. The summer after our mom was shot to death, I was afraid of opening the windows at night, even out here in the middle of the desert. I was afraid that animals and creatures worse than animals would rip open the screens and climb inside, so Grandma sewed the symbol into the center of our quilt.

"Grandma?" I say. "Eva?"

No one replies, except for the fuzzy people on the TV screen. They open and close their misshapen lips, murmuring, begging to be released. Their voices grow louder and more cacophonous. Greenish-yellow flies explode from their mouths.

I turn off the TV and the figures disappear. Honestly, I'm surprised at how easily I can banish them. I always believed that drinking more of the liquid would make the visions more intense. I never thought that my own energies might also augment in some way. Or maybe I was afraid that I couldn't handle this kind of power.

"Hello?" I say, searching my surroundings again. I make eye contact with the large, framed photo of my mother on the wall. Eva and Grandma and I decorated the frame with shells and tiny starfish.

FAMILIAR

"What am I supposed to do now?" I say.

In the photo, Mom smiles at me encouragingly, building a sandcastle with Eva on her left side, and me on her other.

Without thinking, I stand up and walk through the sliding glass door into Grandma's backyard. There is no real yard, however. A small garden is closed off by chicken wire, but everything else is unwalled and untamed. I follow an ill-defined trail created by our own footprints over the summer, weaving my way among the yuccas and apricot mallows and prickly pear cactuses. Up ahead, the smooth branches of a big berry manzanita transform into long, bony fingers. They reach out to me.

"No," I say, and the branches swiftly turn back to normal.

A pair of coyotes with human faces step out from behind a juniper tree. They approach me, wobbling a little, walking on two legs. They bare white, flawless teeth.

"That's enough of that," I say, and the

coyotes lower themselves to four legs. Their faces sprout soft, fulvous fur. Their expressions grow genial and inquisitive. Before Mom was killed, and before I grew frightened of animals, Eva and I used to beg our grandma for a pet coyote. We laughed when we said this. Grandma said that coyotes wouldn't be happy to be put on a leash, or to eat dog food from a bowl. At night, Eva told me stories about us and our trusty pet exploring a magic forest of impossibly-high trees and talking to mushrooms and giant salamanders.

I don't know where I'm going, but it's not long before I reach my destination.

As I approach the boulder, the world around me grows dim, every plant and animal burgeoning with shadows. These shadows expand and touch one another until everything is black.

Darkness has always comforted me.

Getting on my hands and knees, I crawl through the small opening in the boulder and enter what Eva and I call the Cave.

"Eva?" I say, into the darkness.

She doesn't respond. She must not be here.

Once I crawl beyond the small opening of the Cave, I can stand up. There's room enough in this hollow for two small girls, and a little plastic table, and our treasure chest. I search the Cave with the blazing blue beam of my flashlight. I see our paintings on the cave walls of pirates and castles and a few of Grandma's strange swirls to keep us safe.

Then I can feel my heart pounding in my ears, because I spot Gordon. He smiles at me, revealing a mouth full of broken teeth. Blood trickles from his split bottom lip. His teeth chatter as if he's freezing.

"Jesus," I say. "What happened to you?"

As soon as the words escape my lips, I can feel my face heating up with embarrassment. I know what happened. Marcus happened.

"You should eat something," I say.

I open up the treasure chest and poke

around among the chipped teacups and wooden swords and a map drawn in purple crayon. Hidden at the bottom of the chest, I find a bag of barbeque chips.

When I hold out a chip, Gordon closes his mouth into a straight line. So I toss the snack onto the Cave floor for the nocturnal insects.

"Is there anything I can do?" I say.

Gordon responds with a small, melancholic smile. He's becoming slightly transparent. As powerful as I am with all the liquid inside me, we're already losing our grip on each other. He believes this dream is a final goodbye.

"Don't think that way," I say. "I'll find a way to bring you back to us."

Gordon's expression shifts, and his grim frown emits an energy that prickles my skin. He feels like a thunderstorm. He's afraid.

I say, "So you already know how I can bring you back. Is that it? You don't want to tell me."

Thunder groans somewhere above as

Gordon keeps his lips pressed tightly together.

"Tell me," I say.

Gordon refuses.

Instinctively, I breathe in deeply, pulling his secrets out of him, the truth filling me uncomfortably like too much air in my lungs.

EVA REACHES OUT towards the line of ducklings with tawny puffball heads. Wiggling her fingers, she says, "Come to me, floofy babies. I need to eat you all up. Come on."

The ducklings glide swiftly away.

"Maybe next time," Eva says.

We continue circumnavigating the lake, and Eva always remains a few feet ahead of me. She's moving too quickly. She's gesturing more than usual when she speaks.

Eventually, the catfish appear, and for a while they follow us at the edge of the water, opening and closing their mouths. I can hear them whispering in my mind, somehow. I can sense their impulses.

"I don't have anything for you," Eva says. "Sorry."

The catfish continue whispering.

Eva then speedwalks over to our favorite bench, and once I catch up with her, she says, "This is exactly what I needed. This is heaven."

"It really is," I say.

She stares out at the lake, her face checkered with the shadows of moving trees.

"Marcus was never right for you," I say.

She glances at me and says, "I don't want to talk about Marcus right now."

"Sorry."

After a few seconds of silence, she says, "Marcus is afraid. That's all this is." She picks up a leaf that landed on her shoulder and begins to roll it up. "If he wants to throw away everything we've built together because of his fear, I can't stop him. But I think this freakout is only temporary."

"Maybe so," I say.

Eva holds the rolled-up leaf to her eye and peeks through the hole, out at the water. Then she tosses the leaf onto the ground.

"Let's talk about something else," she says. "Let's pretend that we're us from four years ago. That was a good era."

"Okay," I say.

She picks up another leaf from off the bench and rips it in half. "This already breaks my own rule, but did I ever tell you about the manicurist I met out here maybe two years ago? She was retired, but she used to be a manicurist. She wore these red, super pointy, cat-eye sunglasses and a silk scarf with a train pattern. Old-timey trains." Eva continues ripping at the leaf. "She reminded me of Grandma a little, the way she could strike up a conversation without any hesitation or awkwardness. She made me feel like we were old friends." Without looking down, Eva sprinkles the leaf pieces onto the ground. "We walked together for a while, talking about this and that. I can't remember how we got on the topic, but at one point we were looking out at the water, and she told me that every lake in the world has a monster. She said that when a man-made lake like this one is created, there aren't any spare monsters who can come here and fill the position. So a new monster has to be created. She said that no one quite knows what the monster looks like yet, because he's still being formed." Eva cups her hands together and breathes warm air into them. "The woman said that in the town where she was born, her monster would lure pregnant women to the edge of the water and then pull them inside. The monster would attach a series of suction cups to the woman's stomach and suck out the soul of the unborn baby. Sometimes the mother drowned. Sometimes she was pushed back out of the water alive. Without a soul, the babies always died." She takes a deep breath. "The manicurist, and I can't believe I still can't remember her name, asked me how I pictured our monster. She wanted to hear everything, so I let loose. I said that to me, the monster's a giant salamander. She's red with white flecks, like a fly agaric mushroom. She has round, black river stones for eyes, and a wide, wide grin. She's not interested in devouring souls or babies. However, I imagine that she's not all bug hunting and smiles. I don't know if you remember this, but when we were in elementary school, we told Victoria that we'd throw her in the lake if she didn't leave us alone. She kept throwing sand in our hair. We told her the salamander would bite off her big toe. Do you remember that?"

"Sort of," I say.

Eva rubs her hands together and then retracts them into the sleeves of her shaggy jacket. "I told the manicurist that the salamander might eat a toe from time to time. She would leave a girl like Victoria alone, I think, but if someone were out on a boat attacking someone else, the salamander would probably intercede. She'd swim at the boat, faster than a dolphin, and headbutt the hull, knocking him into the water. As the guy treads water, the salamander would bite the guy's toe off, or his whole foot. I told the manicurist that the salamander would also save someone from drowning. Her skin is moderately toxic, so she would have to hurry, and swim the person to safety as quickly as possible. She tries, sometimes, to will her body not to secrete those toxins from her glands, but she can't control that part of herself. Anytime a human touches her, her body reacts. She's aware that there are some humans out there who would kill her, if given the opportunity. They'd kill her just because she existed." She breathes into the holes of her sleeves, one after the other. "After I told the manicurist all this, she patted my arm a little, the way Grandma used to do, and said that the salamander sounds nice enough as far as monsters go. She told me to keep the salamander in my heart, because maybe with my help, the monster in the lake wouldn't form into something too bad. Can we keep walking? I need to move."

"Okay," I say, and we continue forward.

After a moment, a frisbee whizzes by my head and a disembodied voice shouts, "Sorry."

"We parted ways after that," Eva says. "Me and the manicurist. I think her name was a kind of flower or tree. Something like that. Anyway, after she left, I kept walking for a while and I thought a little more about the monster. I pictured her at the bottom of the lake, only she wasn't a salamander. She was a heap of wriggling organs, connected by little tendrils of red flesh. Someday she would take her true form, but at that point she was only half-finished and half-alive. She felt so real in that moment. For a second or two, I considered actually swimming to the bottom of the lake and speaking to her in the waking world. But the moment passed. The water was too cold anyway." She shivers. "Are you ready to head back? I'm an icicle."

"I'm ready."

Back in the warmth of the apartment, the two of us sit side-by-side, watching TV and sharing our snacks, the way we've always done since we were little. Ordinarily, Eva talks over the characters. She tells me what she thinks will happen in the show, and what she thinks should happen. Right now, however, she's noiseless. She's hardly laughing or eating. She keeps checking her phone.

When she notices me looking at her, she smiles at me so that I won't worry.

This is the moment when I finally make my decision.

Without speaking, I head over to the far side of the living room and place my palm against the unpainted patch of drywall. I reach out through a small sliver in the wall. Using a scrawny, quivery part of my soul, I reach across the oscillating landscapes beyond. Violet eyestalks growing in a field glance up at me. A moment later, the eyeballs unfurl themselves into spirals of filamentous flesh that stretch in my direction. I speed through storm clouds made from kaleidoscopic gasses and cobwebs of electricity. The storm sprays me with harmless sparks, as a sort of greeting, maybe, or a joke. "Hi," I say, and I progress forward. I reach through contorting towers of vibrating bones and luminescent tendons. As the towers bend and flex at various joints, the tendons tighten and loosen, producing different tones. There's no harmony to the music, but it is music.

I journey on and on, and with every passing moment, I can feel myself growing thinner. The scrawny, quivery part of my soul is the strongest part of me, and the most vulnerable. What if I stretch myself too thin, and break myself in two?

"This was a great plan," I say. "I definitely thought this through."

As I travel deeper, the landscapes become even more amorphous and disorienting. There's no longer any up or down. I squeeze myself through narrow tunnels of undulating flesh and bursting colors.

Finally, I come to a small room that smells like roses and ozone. There's furniture here, in a sense. A series of interlocking bones protrude through the fleshy floor in the shape of a coffee table. An enormous blister bulges beside the table, looking mildly couchlike. Nearby, there's also a recliner made from silky purple hair. This is our apartment.

"Gordon," I say, although I can't see him anywhere. Maybe this whole place is him.

After a moment, he appears in the wall as his usual mouth.

I expect an apocalyptic frown, as Eva would say. Instead, his mouth simply goes slack, and he emits an energy like cold, drizzly rain.

"I'm sorry," I say.

He deserves more than a simple apology, but there's no time for anything else. I can already feel myself disappearing.

And so I reach out and touch him gently on his upper lip, giving him back everything Marcus took from him. His teeth clatter together, rhapsodically. He can't help himself, I know. He's like a dog wagging his tail.

When I release him, my essence retracts into itself like a tape measure, and I'm back home, touching the unpainted drywall. I hear my body smack against the floor, more than I can feel it. Through my closed eyelids, I watch as threads of violent flesh twirl around my arms and legs. They squeeze my skin, tighter with every passing moment. Deep inside me, my veins and arteries transmute into a complex latticework of electricity. All the while, the discordant vibrations of the skeletal towers hum in my ears.

"Char!" Eva says, from somewhere nearby. "Char!"

As darkness enwraps me like a warm quilt, my last wakeful thoughts are that I am not the reasonable one after all and that I am most certainly doomed.

THE MOMENT I sit up in bed, Eva hands me a bowl of Grandma's secret soup. This is the soup Grandma made for us whenever we brushed against a prickly pear cactus during tag or tumbled off a small boulder during a sword fight. I also remember sipping at a mug of secret soup when I couldn't sleep, sitting in the dim living room as Grandma told me stories about girls who lost parents or siblings or pets, and then the children went on to explore caves and fight skeletons and discover magic amulets. Grandma's stories always wove together. The girl who defeated the furry dragon grew up and adopted the circus girl who lost her parents in a fire. The circus girl ended up on a pirate ship captained by the girl who once flew to the moon on the back of a seagull made of light. Eva almost always begged for our coyote to be incorporated into the story. Sometimes Grandma obliged her.

As I think about those days and those stories, I swallow a few spoonfuls of the soup. The spices dance in my head, as my grandma would say. Eva watches me in silence for a while.

Then she says, "How are you feeling?"

"Fine," I say.

Eva stares deep inside me. "I almost called an ambulance after you fainted," she says. "But then Gordon materialized and grinded his teeth and frowned. I've never seen him look so anxious. He didn't want me to call the ambulance." She joins me on the bed, sitting cross-legged with her shoes on. "I tried to get an explanation from him, but you know how nebulous Gordon can be in the waking world. He wasn't exactly comprehensible. From what I can gather, though, he seems to think a medic or a doctor might harm you in some way. Does that make any sense to you?"

"No," I say, and I bring the bowl of soup to my lips.

"He seemed to think you would regain consciousness soon, so I didn't call the ambulance. I decided to trust him. I hope I did the right thing."

What she's really saying is, *Did I do the right thing?*

"I think you did," I say. "Thank you for the soup."

She takes the empty bowl from my hands and balances it on her knee. "Do you need to sleep?"

"No. I'm not tired."

I can tell she's dying to know, so I tell her about the eyestalks and the kaleidoscopic gasses and the bone towers. I tell her about the apartment of blisters and skin and hair that Gordon built because he missed us. I explain that Marcus crushed some of Gordon's knowledge into tiny shards and so I had to show him the way from here to there again. I leave out all the details that would devastate my sister, because I'm not ready to do that yet. Maybe I can keep the truth from her forever.

"That's amazing," Eva says. "You're amazing."

"I'm not," I say.

"Do you need anything else? More soup?"

"No."

"Okay. I'm exhausted. I'm off to sleep a hundred years."

Eva scoots herself off the bed, holding the empty soup bowl with her teeth. Close to the bedroom door, she drops the bowl into her hands and says, "If you figure out why Gordon was freaking out about doctors, let me know, okay?"

"I will."

She leaves me then.

I turn off my lamp and close my eyes, Grandma's secret ingredients dancing in my head, turning in strange spirals. For a few moments, I feel safe, although I know that's not true.

Once I can hear Eva snoring in her bedroom, I crawl out of bed as silently as possible. I grab a tincture bottle from the dish drying rack beside the sink, and I approach Gordon.

"Welcome back," I whisper.

FAMILIAR

He replies with a small smile.

"Do you mind?" I say, holding up the glass bottle.

He continues smiling, and so I hold out the tincture bottle and begin collecting some of the liquid trickling from the corner of Gordon's mouth.

"What's going to happen to me?" I say.

Gordon frowns and chews gently on his bottom lip. He's frightened. He doesn't know what's going to happen. He was afraid for me to enter his realm, because he didn't want his realm to enter me.

Once the bottle fills completely, I screw on the dropper cap.

"I'm sorry I didn't listen to you," I say. "But you belong with us. I had to do something."

Gordon clicks his teeth together affectionately, still frowning a little.

"I'll see you soon."

Before returning to my bedroom, I retrieve the shriveled, severed hand from inside the wooden blanket chest where we keep our treasures.

In bed, I drip twenty drops of liquid into my mouth, and my hand doesn't tremble. The taste of roses and ozone waltzes on my tongue with Grandma's secret spices. I close my eyes, holding the shriveled hand in mine. I feel no repulsion towards the magical object. Gordon might have used Cowboy Hat's organic matter to create the object, but this is not Cowboy Hat's hand any longer. It's more a manifestation of Gordon's thoughts and dreams.

Through my eyelids, I can see Gordon's teeth.

"What does it do?" I say, holding out my palm, the golden veins glimmering inside my semi-transparent skin.

And Gordon shows me.

WE WANDER THE abandoned factory district for an hour and twenty-four minutes before we find a pair of corrugated metal doors skillfully graffitied to look like a face. At the center of each twinkly eye is a round, cloudy window inset in the door. The bent nose hints at an old injury, long-since healed. Chains connecting the door handles resemble a slight frown. In my dream last night, the door spoke to me. He said, "You don't want to come inside me. I'm sick. It feels like the plague." In real life, the door can't speak to me any longer, but he wears the same worried expression.

"Are you sure this is it?" Eva says.

"I'm sure," I say.

"Are we really doing this?"

"I guess we are."

Eva takes a deep breath and then removes the bolt cutters from her pink duffel bag. Using the tool, she cuts through the door's chain lips.

I pull as hard as I can and the door groans open as if to say, "You don't want to do this."

After I take a step forward, Eva wraps her arms around me. She squeezes me tight. I know she means well, but the hug frightens me more than anything. I think Eva believes that we might not survive this hunt. I think I believe that too.

"Everything's going to be fine," I say. "We'll follow the plan and we'll get this done."

"Yeah," Eva says, quietly.

With my phone in one hand and the severed hand in the other, I guide us through the building, as if I know where I'm going. I have traveled these labyrinthine corridors in my dreams, but that only helps so much. I do recognize a few landmarks here and there, like the striped sock hanging from a bent nail, and the graffiti crab in a tutu. I must be going the right way.

FAMILIAR

Every so often, I glance down at my phone and check the time. We've been walking these corridors for two minutes and sixteen seconds. The next time I check, we've been walking for three minutes and forty-two seconds. This is an old habit. This is me focusing on tiny details so that I'm not overwhelmed by the big picture. And this is one big, grotesque picture we've trapped ourselves inside.

"I think we're getting close," I whisper. I can feel tears of sudden terror struggling to escape my face. We should have listened to the door. We should never have come inside him.

Ahead, I see the familiar arched doorway with a soft, yellow light radiating from the chamber beyond. This is it.

Eva touches me on the arm and I jump a little.

"Sorry," she whispers in my ear.

After pocketing our phones, we remove our shoes and then head forward in our gripper socks, as quietly as we can. My heart booms in my ears. Eventually, we pass through the arched doorway, and we reach our destination.

I know this is the right place because dozens of 5-gallon green buckets sit on the cement floor. A paper-mache face covers the top of each bucket, the paper-mache mouths wide open. The faces are striped and brightly-colored, like clowns or tropical fish. Strings of golden fairy lights dangle from above, held to the ceiling with duct tape.

We move deeper into the chamber, careful not to disturb the buckets or the lights.

Suddenly, a blur of color rushes through an open door on the opposite side of the room. He sprints towards Eva, but then freezes in place. He stares entranced at the withered eyeball in Eva's hand.

"Jesus," I say.

In my dream, he was nothing but a blur. In real life, he's a man in his thirties, I think, dressed in jeans, a black t-shirt, and a canvas apron. He's holding a sizable hunting knife with a serrated edge.

Brightly-colored paint speckles both his hands. The fingers gripping the knife twitch slightly.

"Jesus," I say again.

Before I can say anything else, the man charges forward and stabs Eva in the stomach. She gasps almost imperceptibly before he kicks her to the floor. Her head slams into one of the buckets, causing the paper-mache face to tumble away. A swarm of flies escapes from the bucket.

"Damn it," the man says. "What a fucking mess."

He faces me now, still gripping the hunting knife. The blade drips with my sister's blood.

I point the magical hand at him, and the man moves swiftly. He grabs a bucket from off the floor and swings it at me, knocking the weapon out of my hand.

He comes closer and laughs.

He's only a foot or two away when my left arm blazes with pain. At first I'm worried that he's already stabbed me, but then I notice the violet eyestalks burgeoning from my fingertips. My forearm ripples and squirms and bursts forth with fleshy knots. I force myself to look away from what's happening to me, turning my attention back to the Bucket Man. He's staring at me with wide eyes. As soon as one of the eyestalks wraps around his neck, he drops the hunting knife.

I pick up the magical, severed hand. I rush forward, concentrating as best I can, and I poke his shoulder with the magical hand's forefinger.

The Bucket Man presses his palms against his face. He screams. His head, his arms, and his legs retreat into his torso, like the extremities of a turtle. For a while, his flesh trembles on the cement and makes a slowly intensifying squelching sound. Then his torso implodes. He ends up as a small ball of flesh with a tiny mouth.

"What the fuck," he says, in a high-pitched voice. "What the fuck. What the fuck."

I rush over to my sister. In all my

visions, she was never stabbed. This wasn't supposed to happen.

"Eva," I say.

Her body shakes as blood streams from her wound. She takes shallow, speedy breaths. Her now-purple lips glisten with sweat.

"What the fuck did you do to me?" the Bucket Man says.

"Quiet," I say.

The Bucket Man's tiny lips seal together.

I turn my attention back to Eva. I need to stop the bleeding. I need to call an ambulance. Or is it already too late?

After a moment of consideration, I hold out the magical, severed hand and touch her shoulder. Her body instantly caves in on itself and shrinks and condenses.

A few seconds later, I pick her up in my hand. At this point, I notice that my left arm's back to normal now. The eyestalks and fleshy knots are gone.

"Eva?" I say. "Can you hear me?"

"Yeah," she says, in a small, high-pitched voice.

"How do you feel?"

"Like a weird little ball of flesh without any eyes. But the pain's gone, so that's a plus. What do we do now?"

How do I tell her that I don't have a plan? How do I tell her that this moment feels more dreamlike and disorienting than any vision I've ever experienced? How do I tell her that I can feel Gordon's realm whorling inside my chest, aching to express itself through my body again? What if next time the eyestalks and the knots overwhelm me?

"We'll figure something out," I say.

I gather together the severed hand and the withered eyeball and Eva's shoes. I place them all inside the duffel bag, along with the Bucket Man. As for Eva, I carry her carefully in my right hand. I'm careful not to squeeze her too tight.

"How are you feeling?" I say.

"Fine," she says. "Strange."

According to my visions, there aren't

any survivors in the next room with the metal tables and the saws and the paint supplies, but I search there anyway. My visions were correct.

Before leaving, I remove the paper-mache faces from off the buckets, and I free the flies. It's a silly thing to do, but I can't help myself.

"Are you still doing okay?" I say.

"Yes," Eva says. "You don't have to keep asking me every five minutes."

"Sorry."

With my sister in my right hand, and my phone in the left, I move quickly through the tortuous corridors, pretending to myself that I remember the way back.

GORDON HOLDS THE Bucket Man's round body between his lips the way a child might suck on a large jawbreaker. Every so often, Gordon puckers his lips and makes a slurping sound.

"You can talk now," I say, and the Bucket Man's mouth materializes again.

"What did you do to me?" he says, in his cartoonish voice. "What the fuck are you?"

"We don't owe you any explanations." I close my eyes and focus on that scrawny, quivery part of my soul that can still feel all the pain of my mother's death. "You don't want to harm anyone else," my pain says.

"I don't want . . . " the Bucket Man says. "I . . . what the fuck are you doing to me?"

"You don't want to harm anyone else," Eva says, nestled on a pillow on the coffee table.

Gordon gnaws on the Bucket Man, slurping louder than before, breaking down his walls and absorbing pieces of his flesh the way he took Cowboy Hat's arm.

"I'll kill you when I get out of this," the Bucket Man says. "You came to me in the transfiguration room because I'm meant to transmute your sins into flies. I am destined for—"

"You're destined for nothing," I say. "All your rationalizations for killing are bullshit. Every time you think of them, you realize they're bullshit."

"They're not bullshit," he says, sounding more than a little offended.

"They are."

"They are," he says.

"You kill because you like to."

"That's true."

I lean forward, and project my words into his soul. "You don't want to harm anyone else."

"Please," the Bucket Man says. "Please just let me kill Angelina. I've been preparing for her for so long. Years. She's admitted so much to me. She texts me every day. Let me kill her, and then I promise I'll—"

"You don't want to harm anyone else," I say.

"You don't want to harm anyone else," Eva says, behind me.

"I don't want to harm anyone else," the Bucket Man says.

"You won't remember us," I say. "But our words will live in your soul until the day you die."

"Until I die," he says.

With that, Gordon spits out the Bucket Man, and I catch the ball of flesh in my outstretched hands. I return him to the pink duffel bag.

Goosebumps spread across my arms when I turn to Eva. This might be the worst idea of all time. I should probably take her to the hospital, and then turn her back with the magical hand, and then let the doctors try to save her. But what if they can't?

"Are you ready?" I say.

"I think so," she says.

And so I pick up the ball of Eva and slide her into Gordon's open mouth, on top of his wide, indigo tongue. He closes his lips over her.

"Be careful with her," I say, although I know he will. He adores Eva more than anything in the world, just like me.

Gordon rolls Eva around in his mouth like a fine wine. After a while, I realize that I'm holding my breath.

I let myself breathe. I need to calm myself, because I can feel the energies of Gordon's realm convulsing inside me, attempting to take shape again.

"How's it going, Gordon?" I say.

He doesn't respond. He's probably too focused to even hear me.

Sitting on the couch, I tell myself that Eva's going to be fine, and it feels like a lie.

I wait. I pray to whoever or whatever's listening that Gordon harvested enough organic matter from the Bucket Man to rebuild Eva. Gordon doesn't understand the intricacies of the human body, and he's not a healer. Gordon didn't seem too confident when I proposed the idea.

I wait. I think about the time when we

were little, and we were playing a game of hide-and-seek in Grandma's backyard, and I couldn't find her anywhere. Eventually, I told Grandma, and we searched for her together. We called her name, over and over. I'd never heard Grandma shout so loud. The sound of her voice frightened me.

Finally, we found Eva standing near a colossal yucca palm, with a serpentine scratch on her arm, and a stick in her hand. "I got lost," she said, before we even asked her a question. I remember the rattled look on her face.

At last, Gordon opens his lips and presses Eva partway out of his mouth.

"Are you done?" I say.

Gordon offers me a small, nervous smile.

I pluck the little frowning blob of Eva out of his mouth and place her gingerly on the couch.

"How do you feel?" I say.

"Fine," Eva says.

"Should we try now?"

FAMILIAR

"Yeah."

I grab the severed hand from off the coffee table, and I concentrate, and I touch Eva with the glowing forefinger.

After a second, the small ball explodes in a chaotic cluster of flesh and bone and skin and hair. The pieces of her rearrange themselves until, all at once, she's herself again. She's naked, and she's missing her right hand, and her right ear is now a bizarre fractal of flesh. What's important, though, is that the wound in her stomach is gone.

"Well, that was fun," Eva says.

"Shut up," I say, handing her one of the microfiber blankets that she loves. "Are you in any pain?"

"Nope," she says.

She wraps herself up in the blanket, and I hug her. There's so much I want to tell her.

"I'll be right back," she says. "Oh, and thank you, Gordon. You saved my life. Thank you."

Gordon clicks his teeth together, joyously.

Eva glides into her bedroom, and I sit on the couch, wiping at my tears with my knuckles.

A couple minutes later, Eva returns dressed in her fuzzy pink jacket and black pants.

I know Eva's not one for licking her wounds, but I still expected her to rest for a while. I expected a pizza night and homemade margaritas and bad crime shows.

"I'll go drop him off," Eva says.

"Him?" I say. "The Bucket Man?"

"Yeah." She tosses the severed hand into the duffel bag.

"Are you sure about this?" I say.

She zips up the bag. "I won't hurt him, if that's what you're worried about."

"That's not what I'm worried about. You almost died, Eva."

"Exactly." Still standing, she wiggles her feet into her tennis shoes. "He almost killed me. I need to go out there and remind myself that he didn't. We won. He's no longer a threat. I'll be back in a bit."

After grabbing the duffel bag, she disappears out the door.

FAMILIAR

I stand staring at the door for a while, worried that Gordon may have taken away something vital from the Bucket Man. What if he took more than some blood and an appendix? What if when Eva zaps the Bucket Man back to normal, he dies from a missing heart or a hollow skull?

No, Gordon wouldn't do that. He's not interested in vengeance. He's all about mitigating pain and suffering. Isn't he?

I approach the wall, feeling guilty for all these thoughts.

"Thank you," I say.

Gordon smiles at me.

The truth of what happened with the eyestalks and the fleshy knots struggles to escape my throat, but I stop myself from speaking. I'm too exhausted to deal with this right now.

And after all, Eva is right. We won. Maybe I can celebrate by lying down on the couch and eating some barbecue chips and for a couple hours not contemplating the nameless horrors hatching inside me. That would be nice.

Tonight's the night, supposedly.

Gordon won't give us any hints about this mystery gift of his. When I bring up the subject, he only smiles a cryptic smile, even in my dreams.

Fists of wind and rain slam against the windows, but even they can't drown out Eva's herculean snoring. She's splayed out on her velvety, purple recliner, the microfiber blanket wound up around one leg. The sight of her fractal ear and her missing hand doesn't worry me the way it once did. Early on, I panicked about what losing her dominant hand might mean in her life, but she's coping well. Of course she is.

I glance over at Gordon. At this point, his mouth's impossibly wide, like some out-of-proportion gargoyle. He must be close. How much wider can his mouth get?

While I'm waiting, I half-watch an episode of our usual show where the British puppeteer transforms a group of department store mannequins into makeshift marionettes. He needs to convince a specific clerk that the mannequins are alive and hungry for blood. I haven't paid enough attention to know why. Partway through the episode, a fidgety sort of ache travels up and down my left arm.

I massage my left palm a little with my other hand and say, "Okay."

After taking a few deep breaths, I don't so much command my hand to change as gently suggest some new looks. With my thoughts, I propose fingers covered with nacreous scales, the colors of abalone shells. I propose that gossamer, cherry-red feathers should sprout from my forearm. I propose the idea of talon-like fingernails, stronger than stone.

My ideas immediately come to pass, more or less. The feathers are more orange than red. The scales are larger than I had in mind. What's most important, however, is that the transformations hardly cause me any pain these days.

"Looks good," I whisper, admiring our collaboration.

Seconds later, my hand turns back to normal, although normal is probably not the right word. I'm still shocked at how things have changed these past couple months. When I first told Gordon what happened to my arm in the Bucket Man's bucket room, Gordon was terrified. His terror intensified my own. He feared for my life, because his realm is nothing if not unpredictable. I'm sure he believed I was one strong sneeze away from exploding.

Eva, meanwhile, didn't panic at the news. I told her while we were waiting together at a fast-food drive-through, and she hardly blinked. Always the optimist, she suggested that I talk to the energies in my arm and try to work things out.

And so, late at night, as drowsiness closes in on us from all sides, I'll tell the energies my anxieties and my fears. I'll tell them about a customer who yelled at me because she was offended by a charity flyer on the wall that includes the word testicular. I'll tell them my worries about Marcus and his reemergence into my sister's life. I would never speak so bluntly with Eva, but the truth about Marcus is that he's superficial. I think he loves Eva because of her face and her body. I think if he'd found Gordon aesthetically pleasing, he wouldn't have smashed him with a mallet. Of course, I might be completely wrong about Marcus. I don't have the best instincts when it comes to human beings. And after telling my left arm these things, the energies will speak to me of their own anxieties. They'll show me a whirlpool of light that freezes in place and never moves again. They'll show me a tunnel of muscle tissue that spins clockwise and counterclockwise simultaneously. We can't always understand each other, but we can empathize. We're both worriers.

I still don't understand what's happening to me, but contemplating these little details makes me feel a little better.

On the TV, the puppeteer manipulates the ropes, causing two headless mannequins to embrace. I curl up on the couch. With my eyes half-closed and out of focus, I can't tell the difference between the mannequins and the people on the screen.

If I'm not careful, I'll fall asleep and then I might miss Gordon's special surprise. I don't want to disappoint him. What will it be this time? A kidney that can make you sprout wings and fly? A big toe that whispers cosmic secrets under the full moon?

Thunder booms, and Eva says in her sleep, "But I already paid."

I'm almost asleep when I hear a squishing sound coming from the far wall.

I sit up and look over.

"Eva," I say. "Eva. He's starting. Eva."

"What?" she says.

"It's happening."

Eva sits up and rubs her face with her hands, smearing her makeup.

We watch as Gordon works to disgorge his new top-secret gift.

What pushes through the opening first is a face of soft, fulvous fur.

"What the fuck," Eva says.

A genial grin spreads across the furry

face, revealing a mouth of large, light-blue teeth.

"Gordon?" Eva says.

This new body continues to squeeze out of the wide-open mouth, and finally he plops onto our faux hardwood floor, covered with a thick coating of the golden liquid. He stands up, his legs wobbly.

"Gordon?" Eva says again.

And he shakes his fur and then trots over to us, his elongated face beaming. He's still covered with the liquid, but we pet him anyway. He licks our hands with his prickly, indigo tongue. As I pet him, a feeling like static electricity frolics on my palm. I can feel our energies intermingling and intensifying. We're stronger all together like this. I see now that Gordon could never truly connect with us when he was trapped in the wall.

"How the hell did you crawl out of your own mouth?" Eva says, and laughs.

Gordon makes a sound reminiscent of a bark. This is the first sound he's ever produced, aside from slurps and smacks and clicks.

At this point, lightning illuminates the room, and for a second, I see our spirits or whatever exists inside us light up like stars. Touching each other, we form a sloppy constellation of our own creation. As soon as the lightning fades, so does the vision. But the meaning remains, rumbling like a thunderclap inside me.

As we cuddle together in our dim living room, we're also standing at the top of the high-rise apartment tower, blessed by a swirling, blazing universe, our bodies made of crimson flowers and chrysocolla stones and dead painted lady butterflies. We're here. We made it. It was silly of me, but I thought that reaching these heights would make me feel exceedingly confident, and powerful, and free. But truth be told, I'm more frightened than ever.

After all, we're standing at the edge of an impossibly-high precipice. The scrawny, quivery part of my soul says that the blurred men we've faced are nothing compared to the dangers to come. But my family is also dangerous.

FAMILIAR

Maybe we can survive this. Maybe we can even change the world a little. And if we can't, well, at least it was a beautiful dream.

ABOUT THE AUTHOR

Jeremy C. Shipp is the Bram Stoker and Shirley Jackson Award-nominated author of *The Atrocities, The Merry Dredgers,* and *Cursed*. Their shorter tales have appeared in over 60 publications, including *Cemetery Dance* and *Apex Magazine*. Jeremy lives in Southern California, and until recently they believed a pony was a baby horse. You can learn other important facts about Jeremy at jeremycshipp.com.

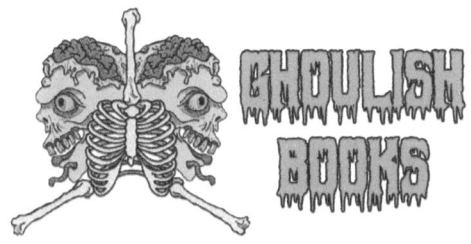

Patreon:
www.patreon.com/ghoulishbooks

Website:
www.Ghoulish.rip

Facebook:
www.facebook.com/GhoulishBooks

Twitter:
@GhoulishBooks

Instagram:
@GhoulishBookstore

Linktree:
linktr.ee/ghoulishbooks

www.ingramcontent.com/pod-product-compliance
Lightning Source LLC
Chambersburg PA
CBHW011509170626
46812CB00009B/3031